# The Berenstain Bears' Graduation Day

The old school year
is passing.
We've put our books away.
It's a time for hope and
memory—
on graduation day.

Diploma

Brother Bear is hereby
Promoted from Third
to Fourth Grade

Signed *Principal Honeycomb*

## Mike Berenstain

### Based on characters created by Stan and Jan Berenstain

**HARPER FESTIVAL**
*An Imprint of HarperCollinsPublishers*

The Berenstain Bears' Graduation Day Copyright © 2014 by Berenstain Publishing, Inc.
All rights reserved. Manufactured in China.
No part of this book may be used or reproduced in any manner whatsoever without written permission except in the case of
brief quotations embodied in critical articles and reviews. For information address HarperCollins Children's Books, a division of
HarperCollins Publishers, 195 Broadway, New York, NY 10007.
Library of Congress catalog card number: 2013950472
ISBN 978-0-06-207555-0

14   15   16   17   SCP   10  9  8  7  6  5  4  3
❖
First Edition

Spring was nearly over in Bear Country. The daffodils and tulips had come and gone. So had Easter candy and Mother's Day cards. June was about to arrive, and for Brother and Sister Bear that meant just one thing: *no more school!*

Sister was finishing first grade and Brother was moving up from third. Even little Honey was ending her first year of day care.

They all learned a lot in school that year. Brother's class studied the Earth and learned about rocks, earthquakes, and volcanoes. He even made a model of a volcano that squirted lava out the top!

Sister's class learned about plants and animals. They took care of a cute little hamster and kept a lizard and a frog in a glass case full of plants and mossy rocks. They brought cocoons in from the cold to watch as beautiful butterflies and moths hatched out of them.

Honey learned things, too. She played with toys that taught about shapes and numbers. She learned how to do things with other cubs.

But she did not need to learn how to take naps.

She was already good at that.

The cubs did other fun things at school, too. They played sports like soccer, basketball, and baseball. They played games during recess.

They went on exciting field trips to interesting places.

The cubs enjoyed their school year. But they were ready for a break. They were looking forward to summer—to picnics and swimming, to hiking and fishing, to long summer evenings of chasing fireflies and toasting marshmallows.

When the month of May came to an end, it was time to turn the calendar to June. The cubs drew a big red circle around the last day of school and crossed off each day as it passed.

This year, the Bear Country School was having a real graduation ceremony for every grade in the school. Mama and Papa thought this was a nice idea. It would make everyone stop and think about how much the cubs had learned and done during a whole year of school.

"Best of all," said Sister, "we get to wear cute graduation costumes!"
"Ugh!" said Brother. "I don't want to look cute."

At last, graduation day arrived and the cubs put on their costumes. They each had a little cap and gown. Even Brother had to admit they didn't look too bad. Brother's was blue. Sister's and Honey's were white. The caps had tassels that kept getting in the cubs' faces. They tried to blow them out of the way.

Grizzly Gramps and Gran stopped by to take pictures.
"My, aren't they adorable!" said Gran, wiping away a tear.
"Time we got going, young 'uns!" said Gramps, looking at his watch. "You don't want to be late for your own graduation day."

When the family arrived at school, the auditorium was packed with the families of graduating students. Then the school band began to play. They played good and *loud*!

The graduating cubs in their caps and gowns marched down the aisle and up onto the stage.

"Look!" said Gran. "There's Brother, Sister, and Honey!"

Gramps stood on his chair to take a picture.

"Get down from there before you hurt yourself!" scolded Gran.

Principal Honeycomb made a few brief remarks. Then Ferdy Factual, one of the best students in the school, gave a speech about honesty, hard work, good sportsmanship, caring for others, and being true to yourself.

"That's Professor Actual Factual's nephew," Mama whispered to Gran.

Papa and Gramps fell asleep. Mama and Gran poked them awake.

Sportsmanship
Hard Work

Finally, all the students filed across the stage as their names were called. Principal Honeycomb handed them their diplomas—fancy rolled-up pieces of paper with their names on them. Gramps stood up on his chair to take pictures again, as Brother, Sister, and Honey received their diplomas. As they marched back down the aisle, cameras flashed and the audience clapped and whistled. Gramps even honked on a loud noisemaker.

Diploma
Brother Bear is hereby
Promoted from Third
to Fourth Grade
Signed Principal Honeycomb

Outside in the schoolyard, the graduating cubs laughed and cried, hugging one another and posing for pictures. They wouldn't be all together again until the next school year.

Too-Tall Grizzly took off his cap and called, "All together now! One, two . . . THREE!" he yelled, throwing his cap into the air.

All the cubs threw their caps in the air. They made a pretty blue-and-white cloud.

"YAAAAY!" the cubs all yelled.

Honey took off her little white cap, too.
"One, two . . . FREE!" she called, throwing it in the air.

"I didn't know Honey could count," said Gran.
"She learned this year in day care," said Papa. "That's what graduation day is all about—being proud of everything our students did in school this year."
"And being excited about all the wonderful things they will be doing next year!" added Mama.

Gramps took another picture.
"Squeeze in closer and say, 'Honey!'" he said.
"Honey!" they all said as the camera clicked.